W9-BCC-396

The Story Of
WILLIAM PENN

Written and Illustrated by Aliki

SIMON & SCHUSTER BOOKS FOR YOUNG READERS
Published by Simon & Schuster
New York London Toronto Sydney Tokyo Singapore

SIMON & SCHUSTER BOOKS FOR YOUNG READERS
Rockefeller Center
1230 Avenue of the Americas
New York, New York 10020
Copyright © 1964 by Aliki Brandenberg
Copyright renewed © 1992 by Aliki Brandenberg
First Simon & Schuster edition 1994.
SIMON & SCHUSTER BOOKS FOR YOUNG READERS is a trademark of Simon & Schuster.
Also available in a HALF MOON BOOKS paperback edition.
The text for this book is set in New Aster.
The illustrations were done in water color and ink.
Manufactured in the United States of America.

10 9 8 7 6 5 4 3 2 1

Library of Congress Cataloging-in-Publication Data
Aliki. The story of William Penn/written and illustrated by Aliki. p. cm.
1. Penn, William, 1644-1718—Juvenile literature. 2. Pioneers—Pennsylvania—
Biography—Juvenile literature. 3. Quakers—Pennsylvania—Juvenile literature.
4. Pennsylvania—History—Colonial period, ca. 1600-1775—Juvenile literature.
[1. Penn, William, 1644-1718. 2. Quakers. 3. United States—History—Colonial
period, ca 1600-1775.] I. Title. F152.2.P4A44 1994 974.8'02'092—dc20 [B]
93-26289 CIP 0-671-88558-8 (HC) 0-671-88646-0 (PBK)

For

Dean
Jamie
Maria Nicole

and
all the other children of
Philadelphia

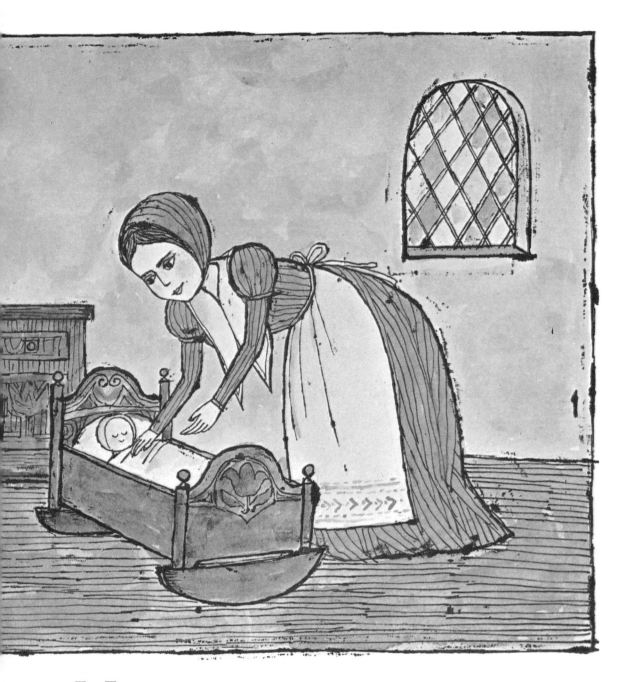

Many years ago there lived a man all the world grew to know. His name was William Penn.

William lived in England with his wife and children, whom he dearly loved.

William's kindness and wisdom won him many friends. Some of them were ordinary people. Some were noble. One was the king of England himself, Charles II.

Although William was wealthy, he did not choose the frivolous life of the rich. He wore no frills as they did. He was a simple man who admired others for their good deeds and not for what they owned.

William was a Quaker. The Quakers are gentle, peaceful people. They do not believe in fighting. They think that all people should live together in harmony.

But in those days, in England, people were not free to say what they chose. They had to speak carefully, or they were punished. Those who did not obey were sent to prison.

William Penn was not afraid. He spoke to the people and told them to believe as they wished. He wrote books and traveled to other countries, telling everyone about freedom.

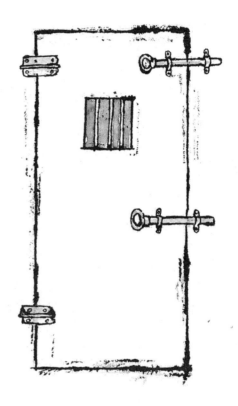

William, too, was sent to prison for a while because he spoke so freely. Yet he never lost hope that all men and women could live together in harmony.

As the years passed, more and more people grew to know and respect William Penn and to believe in his ideas.

Now King Charles happened to owe William a huge sum of money. When the king finally paid his debt, he gave William a large piece of land in America instead of the money.

William had heard of the New World, and of those who went there to seek a better life. He had long dreamed of going there himself.

William set to work, finding others to go with him. He told them that in America they would be free to think and speak as they pleased.

William called his new land Pennsylvania—the woods of Penn.

He planned where a city would be built, and he named the city Philadelphia—the city of brotherly love.

When everything was ready, William bid his family farewell, for they would join him later. The sails were spread and the brave group left their homeland.

The journey was long. The ship moved slowly onward, rocking and tossing on the white-capped waves. Many people fell ill, and everyone wanted the voyage to end.

Two long months passed.

Then one day in 1682 they saw their new land. They saw wigwams nestled among the trees and Native Americans watching them from a distance.

And on the shore stood some earlier settlers, who had come from afar to welcome them.

And they rejoiced.

But the Native Americans, who were called Indians, were uneasy. Many of their people had been chased from their land and hurt by other settlers.

William wanted to make friends with the Native Americans. He did not want them to be afraid of him and of his people, so he invited them to a meeting.

The Indians came, wearing their finest headdresses. Both settlers and natives gave each other gifts in the shade of an old elm tree.

William Penn wrote a Peace Treaty that said:
In this land our two peoples will live
together in respect and freedom.

He proved to all the world that people can live in harmony if they choose.

The Native Americans trusted William because he was fair. He did not chase them from their land but bought it from them.

He visited their homes and respected their customs. He even learned to speak their language and said it was the most beautiful language of all.

William's city grew. More houses were built, and new settlers came in great numbers.

To this day, the father of Philadelphia looks down over his people. And his people look up to him with pride.